To Bob and Margaret ॳ J. E.
For Millie ॳ V. C.

Text copyright © 2006 by Jonathan Emmett
Illustrations copyright © 2006 by Vanessa Cabban

First U.S. edition 2006

Library of Congress Cataloging-in-Publication Data
Emmett, Jonathan.
Diamond in the snow / Jonathan Emmett ; illustrated by Vanessa Cabban. —1st U.S. ed.
p.   cm.
Summary: Entranced by his first snow, Mole explores the white woodlands
and shows his friends the spot where he found a sparkling "diamond."
ISBN-13: 978-0-7636-3117-8
ISBN-10: 0-7636-3117-5
[1. Snow—Fiction. 2. Ice—Fiction. 3. Moles (Animals)—Fiction. 4. Animals—Fiction.]
I. Cabban, Vanessa, date, ill. II. Title.
PZ7.E696Dia   2006
2005055307

2 4 6 8 10 9 7 5 3 1

Printed in China

This book was typeset in Beta Bold.
The illustrations were done in watercolor.

Candlewick Press
2067 Massachusetts Avenue
Cambridge, Massachusetts 02140

visit us at www.candlewick.com

Diamond
in the
Snow

Jonathan Emmett

illustrated by Vanessa Cabban

CANDLEWICK PRESS
CAMBRIDGE, MASSACHUSETTS

"COLD diggety!" gasped Mole
as he burrowed out
of the ground one afternoon.
"Whatever's this?"

It was the middle of winter,
and the woodland was covered
in a thick blanket
of snow.

Mole had never seen snow before.

It made the woodland look strange and beautiful.

So Mole left his hole and set off to explore.

It was SO quiet, as if everything

had fallen under a magic spell.

Mole wandered on, enchanted,

until suddenly . . .

he found
   himself sliding
down a steep
      snowy bank.

"Ooh!"
cried Mole
as his paws slipped
from under him.

"Wheee!"
he shouted
as he sped down
the slope.

"Oooooff f!"
he groaned
as he crashed into
a tree trunk.

Mole picked himself
up—and then gasped
with surprise.
Something smooth
and sparkly was sticking out
of the snow beside him.
Mole was sure that it hadn't been
there a moment ago.

"It's as if it appeared by MAGIC," thought Mole.
"It looks like a diamond," he decided.
"I must take it home!"

Mole carried
the diamond back
up the steep bank.
It was hard work.
The diamond had
become wet
   and slippery
and was
   very difficult
      to hold.

"Drat!"
said Mole
as he stumbled,
and the
   diamond
shot up
out of his
   paws.

"It's as
if it's
trying to escape,"
gasped Mole as he
chased it down
the slope.

"Perhaps it's
a MAGIC diamond,"
he thought.

"Phew!" panted Mole
when he finally reached the top
of the bank. He was HOT and tired,
but he hurried on, anxious to get home.
By now, he was sure that the diamond
was magical, because it was changing shape
in his paws.

He was almost home when he suddenly
realized that his arms were empty.
The diamond had disappeared—
right from under his nose!

Just then, a snowball
came whizzing through the air,
closely followed by Hedgehog,
Squirrel, and Rabbit.

"Hello, Mole," said Hedgehog cheerily.

"Do you want to come snowballing with us?"
asked Squirrel.

But Mole was still staring unhappily
at his empty paws.

"What's wrong, Mole?"
asked Rabbit.

So Mole told them
all about the magic diamond—
how it had appeared from nowhere,
and changed shape and tried to escape—
and how it had finally disappeared
from under his nose.

But Mole could tell that his friends
didn't really believe him. So he took
them back to the tree trunk where
the diamond had first appeared.

"That's where I found it," said Mole,
pointing DOWN into the snow.
Rabbit, Hedgehog, and Squirrel
were all smiling.

"Look," said Rabbit,
pointing UP into the tree.
Mole squinted up—and then he saw them!
The tree above them was filled with
HUNDREDS of diamonds.
They were hanging from every branch.

"They're ICICLES," said Squirrel.

"They're just frozen water," said Hedgehog.

"The one you found must have melted
in your paws," explained Rabbit.

"So it wasn't magic, then,"
said Mole sadly.

"Not really,"
said Rabbit kindly.

The four friends set off
up the bank again. But when they got
to the top, Mole glanced back to take
one last look at the icicle tree.

"Wait a minute,"
he said excitedly. "LOOK!"

The sun was setting
over the snowy woodland,
casting its last rays into the branches
of the tree, making each icicle shimmer
with a beautiful golden light.
It was the most SPECTACULAR thing
any of them had ever seen.

Mole, Rabbit, Hedgehog, and Squirrel stood
staring at the tree, enchanted, until the last
of the light had died away.

"That was MARVELOUS,"
sighed Rabbit as they made their way
back through the woodland.

"WONDERFUL," agreed Hedgehog.

"FANTASTIC," added Squirrel.

"You see," said Mole, grinning proudly.
"I told you they were
MAGIC!"